Photo courtesy of Dr. Aleksey Prok

The author was born in Dover, Ohio in 1957. He graduated from the University of Akron with a degree in Political Science where he was a four-year letterman as a pitcher on the baseball team, while also involving himself in the downtown club scene as a musician. After a brief career as a working musician in Columbus, Ohio Jeff returned to his hometown, where he has pursued his passion for music composition, painting, and writing. His works can be viewed and his music can be downloaded for free by accessing jeffbeitzel.com. Jeff still resides in Dover with his wife, Shelly. They have two grown children, Lee and Blake.

I'd like to dedicate this book to my wife, Shelly, for her positivity and unwavering support of every creative endeavor I undertake.

Jeff Beitzel

sideman

AUSTIN MACAULEY PUBLISHERS™

LONDON • CAMBRIDGE • NEW YORK • SHARJAH

Ordering Information
Quantity sales: Special discounts are available on quantity purchases by corporations, associations, and others. For details, contact the publisher at the address below.

Publisher's Cataloging-in-Publication data
Beitzel, Jeff
sideman

ISBN 9781649798480 (Paperback)
ISBN 9781649798534 (ePub e-book)

Library of Congress Control Number: 2021918402

www.austinmacauley.com/us

First Published 2021
Austin Macauley Publishers LLC
40 Wall Street, 33rd Floor, Suite 3302
New York, NY 10005
USA

mail-usa@austinmacauley.com
+1 (646) 5125767

Acknowledgement

My sister-in-law, J.W. Her invaluable editing input during the process of writing this book was matched only by her support, patience, and often critical analysis which helped me see this book through to the final word.

Jim Gill, Director of the Dover Public Library, for lighting a fire in my belly to make this book a reality.

Tom Flood, for his invaluable technical assistance and friendship.

Everyone at Austin Macauley Publishers, for their professionalism and encouragement throughout the entire publishing process.

Chapter I

It was just another night at a transvestite bar in one of the roughest areas of downtown Columbus, Ohio. Jack Bradley didn't have any reservations about playing a gig anywhere, anytime. He was still a young man after all. The perverse idea of committing suicide by being whacked in a place like this while performing music had a bleak yet romantic notion to it.

The residual effect of a sudden breakup with a girlfriend is sometimes all it takes to put someone in that hole. It's a hole Jack had been in for well over a year since he got the surprise announcement of "last night I kissed someone else." Some guys jump off a bridge, others drive into telephone poles. Jack was going to live as dangerously as possible while indulging himself with the gratifications which come from being a creative artist, damn it. Death by music was it for him.

As fortune would have it, he could play the bass guitar well and was versatile enough to keep himself busy working in the capital city just as it was beginning to explode. It was 1981. This was before the advent of rap. Just before the music ended.

Jack was a shy, skinny white kid from a small town in Ohio and his roots were in blues and jazz. He had never given it too much thought as to why he had gravitated to black music as a teenager when all his classmates were doing the rock thing. Likely, it was due to an iconoclastic rebellious streak that he was going through at that time, and he had yet to rid himself of it. He had been raised in a home that listened to a diversity of music, yet he never considered playing music because he was a ballplayer first and foremost. He could throw a ball before he learned to walk. That was his identity until he made a discovery that would create the duality in him.

It was when he stumbled across a Freddie King record that had obviously been misplaced behind a Mantovani album in a department store that he became hooked on the blues. It was during his sophomore year in high school.

The store manager was kind enough to let customers listen to records before they purchased them, and as soon as Jack heard The Stumble, that was it. He bought the album, and he bought a bass guitar from an old gentleman who charged him all of thirty dollars, throwing in an amplifier on the house. He loved the way the bass established the pulse of a song, creating a bridge between the rhythm, melody and harmony.

Plus, he thought it was cool that he didn't know anyone else who played the bass since everyone seemed to gravitate to the guitar or drums. He began learning to play by ear and developed a facility that allowed him to easily assimilate his style of playing with jazz. That was when he knew he was on to something.

Later, while in college, he played on the baseball team by day and worked the club scene in downtown Akron at night. He kept this a secret, not wanting to risk his scholarship. If his coach found out that he was playing in a whorehouse called the Chat Noir after having pitched in both games of a doubleheader, he would have been shown the door regardless of how well he had performed that afternoon.

After finishing college, which coincided with the unexpected breakup with the girlfriend, Jack had become mired in misery. Not a pleasant fellow to be around. Music was his only salvation. Baseball was in the rearview mirror now.

An old friend from his hometown of Doveland named Bud Dixon offered Jack a place to stay in Columbus until he could find a place of his own and it seemed to be the best place for him to test the waters.

Not long after hitting town, he had lucked into a few club dates around the Ohio State campus, and as a result had come to the attention of a fellow named Neal. Neal Ledbetter was well known among the jazz underground in Columbus as a wealthy slacker who just happened to be a guitar prodigy and a junkie of some renown. It was Neal who had booked the two-night engagement at the bar called My Sister's Place.

Neal was a drug-addled white cat who liked to cop some quick money at a place where he could also score some shit. How he came to choose My Sister's Place was anyone's guess and Jack figured it was none of his business. It's really not your business to know if you're a sideman. Still, this place was not on anyone's radar that Jack knew of.

Upon entering My Sister's Place, one could be mistaken that this was a typical working stiff's joint. It was upstairs, however, where a very unusual private party existed on a nightly basis. Another bar was located above which had a stage at the far end of the room for the band (or whatever debauchery was on tap for that evening). The majority of men in attendance were dressed as women and were roaming around the room, swaying and strutting their best stuff. They were keenly on the lookout for unsuspecting saps to lure with promises of love. Many were actually very attractive, and the lights upstairs were always dimmed for their subterfuge.

As Jack approached the stage, he noticed that most of the band was already there, setting up for the second night. Alvin on keys, a fellow named Bill Menendez on sax and T Witherspoon was going to be the drummer. Neal would be late, as always. Just as Jack was ready to climb the steps to the stage, he was stopped by one of the regulars. "I saw you play last night, whiteboy. I liked what I saw and I still like what I'm seein'. I'll give you whatever action you want. Give it to you for nothin', boy."

Jack was tall and this guy was taller. Tall, slender and super fine to the untrained eye. "Sorry, I got someone else I'm supposed to hook up with later. I appreciate the offer though. Maybe some other time."

"You might change your mind later, boy. Give ya a wang dang doodle on your noodle."

Once onstage, Jack fell into the usual banter that had already begun among the band members as some complimentary drinks arrived from the bar. An unexpected gift.

Apparently, the compliments were from the bartender, who gestured toward the band from behind the bar by raising his martini in salutation before slugging it back, smiling at them with a bemused look of refreshment. Jack turned to his bandmates and muttered, "OK, so maybe tonight won't be so bad after all."

T replied, "That'll depend on our boy, Neal. Don't like the way he's been playin' so loud. Couldn't sleep last night with my ears ringin' like they was. I think this place hates him. He better show some kinda respect or we all might get our asses kicked tonight." Alvin peeked over his piano at Menendez, who was on one knee, pulling a flute from its case. "What the hell ya got there, Bill? Shit, no one'll be able to hear that in here tonight. No way, man. Bad choice."

Menendez just looked at him for a second and then responded, "Neal called me this afternoon and told me to be ready to play Spain tonight. Said he'd make it a feature tune and I've been woodsheddin' all day to get my chops back on this thing."

T shook his head. "I still say this place hates him. And I'll bet you a ten spot that we won't be playin' no Spain."

Raised in affluence, Neal never needed to work. His father's wealth provided him with the privilege of being able to hone his guitar-playing skills while indulging himself by shooting heroin daily. His one additional hobby was kleptomania. At night, he would sneak into the various mineralogy departments on the sprawling Ohio State campus and steal samples. His fascination with the gems which came to both adorn and litter his apartment were nearly as much of a fixation as was his drug habit.

Chapter II

The second night of the freaky deaky show was well underway with the band playing loud as hell. Neal would only play at a loud volume, and he rarely paid attention to the band, making it a problem for anyone unfortunate to work with him because it was difficult to find a groove, which is essential to making a song work with any kind of appreciable cohesiveness.

Also, his penchant for playing bad versions of obscure Stevie Wonder tunes in a jazz/rock fusion fashion was not endearing him to the audience this night. The crowd was already beginning to demonstrate their animosity toward the band and the ridiculous attempts at humor Neal was doling out at their expense between songs.

Voices rang out, "Play some shit we know!" "Somebody put some real music on the jukebox!" "Let Little Lacy get up and sing one!" Little Lacy was not little. She was a very large black woman in a shimmering turquoise dress who sported a massive afro. She was a local from the neighborhood who the regulars obviously had a fondness for, but she was no professional. She sat astride a chair that was turned backward and glared at the band. Jack noticed that her face was contorted into a permanent sneer.

Neal was pretty much in the bag during the second set and was becoming ever more dangerously abusive to the clientele.

"Hey, all you beautiful people. Why'ant you all come back to my place for a Mazzola Oil party? Anyone ever been to a Mazzola Oil party before? Bet ya have!"

Jack could now sense the complete revulsion of the audience toward Neal by witnessing the contempt on their faces. They were glowering at the drunken fool who sported a pompadour and silk shirt as he flashed his gold Rolex at them, reflecting the stage lights into their wincing eyes. He didn't belong there.

The band had pretty much given up trying to accompany the mess and was on auto-pilot for the rest of the night. Menendez had given up during the previous set and was now practicing his flute during the songs, which didn't matter because he was rendered inaudible by the massive volume emanating from Neal's amplifier. Alvin became distracted by one of the more attractive men. "Hey Jack, do you think she'd go out with me?" he asked.

Jack thought he was putting him on. *Shit Al, he's probably got a dong bigger than yours.*

The set ended with a ridiculous version of Doo-Wa Diddy the Boy From New York City which was sung off-key by Little Lacy in an effort to placate the audience. It failed, and Jack couldn't wait to get a drink. One set to go.

Dix the bartender was a good sort. He seemed completely at ease in this environment. A real pro. During the two-night stand at My Sister's Place, Jack had come to regard him as a touchstone of normalcy.

He obviously had a penchant for natty attire, and favored black and white pinstriped shirts with gold armbands that not only went well with his gold teeth, but also gave him the appearance of a croupier at a gaming table in Vegas. Short and stocky in build, he sported scar tissue over both eyes. A sure sign that he had been a boxer at some point in his life. Jack had always been intrigued by the fight game, and so he felt compelled to ask Dix while he was being served his shot and a beer, "You ever have any fights, Dix?"

Dix smiled. "Yeah, man. One just last week in here damn near busted up the joint. Needed to get the cops involved, and it almost cost me my job. Fella who owns this place likes to keep things on the low down, y'know?"

"No, no," Jack said. "I mean like Golden Gloves or pro fights."

Dix smiled again. "Shit man, that was a long time ago. I was a good sparring partner, but I kept getting cut."

"I see," Jack replied.

Dix, reflexively touching his forehead and looking a bit hurt, asked, "Does it really show that much?"

"No, no man," Jack said. "I meant that I understand. I had a friend who was a prospect, but he kept getting head-butted when he sparred and it ruined his chances at being anything other than a good club fighter."

"I see," said Dix.

Now it was the eve of the last set, and Dix leaned forward on the bar with both elbows. In a low voice, he reminded Jack that he'd better watch out because Neal was going to be getting paid after the set. "He's hooked up with a couple bad dudes and there's no tellin' what's gonna happen. Might want to keep your eyes open, y'know?" Jack bought another beer and left a generous tip for Dix's tip.

On the way back to the stage, he caught up with T and told him that he'd better pay attention to Neal once the set ended if he wanted to get paid. "Hey T, let the other fellas know too."

Neal spent the majority of the last set talking to the audience about the damned Mazzola Oil party more and more. They were as unenthused about the idea as they had been before, and their agitation was beginning to swell again. Neal kept it up, slurring insults like a fool with a death wish, creeping closer to inducing mayhem from the increasingly besotted group of transvestites.

During these diatribes, standing on stage as if he were on his own little island, Jack came to realize that these people had feelings. It became apparent to him that even though there are some men who dress like women in order to fool other men into having sex with them, it didn't mean that they deserved Neal's lowbrow attempts at humor at their expense in their own private club.

Chapter III

The final set came to a merciful end, and Jack watched intently as he saw Neal leave the stage and head to the bar where Dix was waiting with the money. Jack timed it so he would arrive seconds later just as the cash exchanged hands and snatched his two night's pay from Neal. Jack could tell by the look on Neal's face that he had indeed thwarted Neal's attempt to make off with the whole take.

By the time Jack hustled back to the stage, T and the others were packing up their gear on the bandstand, and Neal was gone.

"Hey, I told you guys to watch out!" Jack hollered over the sound blasting from the jukebox. He headed downstairs to the unlit parking lot in order to make a quick exit himself. He had his money and the others would have to fend for themselves.

As he made it to his car with his bass in hand, he was spooked by the sudden glare of headlights in his eyes. The headlights belonged to a red Cadillac which was spraying gravel in every direction as it roared toward Jack. Diving for cover as the Caddy passed him with a sense of purpose, Jack noticed a passenger in the back seat. It was Neal, sitting between two big gorillas. One of them was holding a pistol to Neal's head. This was the drug deal that Jack had anticipated and it had obviously gone wrong.

The image of the gun against Neal's head, coupled with the dour expression of dread on Neal's face, provoked a surprised bemusement from Jack as he hunkered in the gravel underneath someone's '73 Buick.

After witnessing that hasty exit, Jack figured he'd make one of his own. He climbed to his feet and unlocked the door of his mustard yellow Volvo station wagon. While clumsily stashing his bass into the back, he heard a scraping, gouging sound and spotted T from across the parking lot. He was working impatiently with a large knife, fully intent on extricating something from the trunk of Neal's luxury sports car. That something turned out to be Neal's guitar, and that guitar was a top-of-the-line model. T smiled a toothy grin at Jack that lit up in the darkness and then he was off with his booty in hand.

Chapter IV

Neal was still alive the next day and was now on the hook to concoct a story to explain to his father why he no longer was in possession of his very expensive instrument. His father was a real estate mogul who, despite his business savvy, was nonetheless a sucker for his son's line of shit. How indignant he became when he was told that a scurrilous drummer had made off with his son's guitar after the previous night's engagement! He had bought that instrument for his son with the sole intention of keeping him focused on not being such a fuck-up.

Subsequently, a police report was filed and poor T was rounded up. When he confessed, he explained in such a convincingly damning way as to why he took the instrument and had it pawned that the police felt it incumbent upon them that they speak to Neal's father about his son.

The next day, a battered Lincoln puttered down one of the most prestigious residential boulevards in the capital city's toniest neighborhood. No house was listed in that neighborhood for under two million dollars, and Neal's dad would know. He developed that allotment and had built his mansion there.

T stopped the Lincoln in the street in front of the Ledbetter mansion, checked the address written on a slip of paper and pulled into the driveway. He exited his car with a feeling of anxiety, noting his surroundings. Everything looked like castles to him. He felt very uncomfortable. Then, remembering that he had business to attend to, he assumed his normal streetwise posture and strode toward the massive oak door of the Montgomery Ledbetter house.

The door opened slowly just as he arrived. T knew that someone had been waiting for him. It turned out to be a distinguished-looking gentleman who stood in the doorway, replete with silk robe and pipe. Neal's dad sure cut an imposing figure. With a dour expression, Monty indignantly thrust his hand across the threshold, displaying two crisp $100 bills. T was ready. Carefully reaching into his shirt pocket, he produced the pawn ticket. While eyeing each other up and down, the slow exchange was consummated.

Observing all this from across the street with more than a small bit of curiosity was a middle-aged man, hiding behind his brick curbside mailbox. He wondered to himself, *What the hell is that? Do I broach the subject with Monty at the club this Wednesday or do I pretend I didn't see this?*

The Lincoln clanked slowly down the long driveway. No words had been exchanged as they are not necessary when two worlds collide. Just one of those incidental things that are cast upon a man who has an aberrant son.

Chapter V

Jack stood holding a bottle of gin in the gravel lot behind Stax's, listening intently as Wilver Jackson went on with his complaining, which arose from the fact that he had two guitar players working with him that night who he felt were indulging themselves at his expense by playing unison lines behind his vocals. He heard this as an intonation problem and the cause of his grievance.

"You can't catch two guitars when you supposed to be playin' one!" Willie looked to the sky as his deep voice resonated with anger. He was sitting on the hood of his pink Cadillac, decked out in his usual vibrant color coordinated three-piece suit with matching derby hat. Tonight's color was yellow.

Physically, he was a dark man from the south, built strong as a bull due to many years spent working the steel mills after having left Chicago years before. He was still working in a mill by day and crooning and catting around at night. Before his Chicago years, he had grown up sharecropping in Mississippi as a boyhood friend of one Elvis Presley. Together they worked the fields around Tupelo and played little league baseball on the same team until Elvis' family uprooted to find work in Memphis and

Wilver Jackson's family headed north. It was in Chicago where Willie had become a blues man, cutting his teeth on the chitlin' circuit with legends such as Elmore James and Muddy Waters.

"Man, when I get with the bass player, that's where my groove's at, you know!"

Jack was a bit surprised by that statement because this was the first time he had met Willie, and he was pretty sure that Willie didn't know that he was a musician, let alone a bassist.

Willie was often surrounded by blues enthusiasts who were always eager to drink or get high with the most popular blues performer in town in-between his sets.

As he passed the bottle of Tanqueray back to his new friend, Jack was tempted to tell Wilver Jackson that he was the main reason he had moved to town. His guitar-playing buddy, Bud Dixon, had whetted Jack's appetite for getting involved in the burgeoning music scene in Columbus. Bud's accounts of having heard a great blues singer who sounded like B.B. King was all it took at that point in time for Jack to get a move on and check it all out. Of course, Jack wasn't going to reveal this to Willie right now. After hearing the last set, Jack knew that he had indeed witnessed the real deal, and he didn't want Willie to think that he was just another blues sycophant.

While passing the bottle with Willie, it dawned on Jack that he was somehow arriving at whatever it was that he was looking for in both music and the vicarious danger that sometimes comes with the territory. It would be just a matter of time now until Willie would drop by a club where

Jack would be playing, and then he could show the great man where his groove was.

Willie was well-loved by everyone due to his penchant for showing up almost anywhere on any given night when he wasn't booked somewhere else in order to just sit in for a couple of tunes and have a nip after a hard day at the mill. He was a man who was totally accessible to his public.

"Damn, and if Warden doesn't stop steppin' on me when I'm tryin' to break it down, I think I'll whup him upside his head some," he continued, referring to one of his problematic guitar players. His large, slightly bulging eyes were wet from drinking. "Sheeeit, might as well finish this bottle and go on in. Doin' it to it."

As they walked toward the back door, he looked over his shoulder and murmured to Jack, "When I get with the bass player, that's where my groove is, you know."

Chapter VI

It didn't take long. Two nights later, Jack was working a basement club on campus, Birdie's. The band he was with that night wasn't entirely bad. The guitar player was Bud, his pal from home who had hipped him to this scene. It was a good, stripped down rhythm section of Jack on bass and Marcus Brown on drums.

The kicker was that the trio had to contend with the likes of a front man in the form of one smallish, egg-shaped, goateed singer/dancer named Big Art. He was the leader. A voracious booker of shitty gigs, usually at strip malls, he occasionally picked up extra money working as a male stripper.

His act consisted of feverish dance moves that often resulted in the inevitable mishaps that befall any white person who foolishly attempts to imitate James Brown, heaven forbid. With this band, which he referred to as Big Art's New Nude Sex Revue, he would work himself into a frenzy which would usually result in Big Art losing his balance and falling into the drum set, wiping out cymbals, drums and sometimes Marcus too. There were tough crowds at those strip malls. Cruel people, starving to get laid. To top it all off, Big Art played the harmonica.

The guys in the band hated it. To them, a harmonica represented many bad memories of having great nights of music flushed down the toilet by some asshole who had asked to sit in with them. The ideal instrument for a blues sycophant. Easy to learn, easy to carry around, and if you can play just a few stock phrases, you can sometimes wheedle your way onto a stage and play pretend. Pretend that you're an actual blues man.

These guys are always white, and usually sport a goatee and beret or some other hipsterish lid. Big Art had the goatee and lid. Jack had always been amazed that guys like that got laid. He knew for a fact that Big Art did when he stumbled across him screwing a chick on the couch where Jack lived with his many derelict housemates in a two-story house just north of campus called Little Bohemia. The poor girl was so embarrassed that she pissed all over Big Art and the couch, which went unused after that. The residents of Little Bohemia somehow couldn't bring themselves to throw the couch away, even though they would never consider sitting on it again. That was left to unsuspecting visitors who didn't notice the stain.

Jack caught a glimpse of Willie coming down the stairs at Birdie's. His heart sank for a moment out of embarrassment because he was in the company of Big Art in his New Nude Sex Revue.

Birdie's had a very low ceiling, as many basement bars do. This was not going to prove to be conducive to Big Art's act at the moment. His penchant for swinging his microphone by its cord like a rodeo cowboy handles a lasso, letting out the cord a little more with each swing, backfired as the microphone smashed into the ceiling lights above, raining glass down upon the entire band. The room broke out in laughter, and then applause because the band kept playing. Jack and the other fellows in the band were also laughing as they continued to grind out the funk while covered in broken glass.

The set ended abruptly after that in order to clean up the mess, and Jack made his way to the bar where Willie sat smiling. There was a beer placed on the bar in front of him and one placed on the bar in front of the empty seat next to him. "Have a seat, young dude." Willie gestured toward the stool. "I see Big Art's gettin' carried away again. Somebody needs to put a gov'nor on his ass." Willie plucked a large shard of glass from Jack's head. "Come on down to the Tropicana on Saturday. And don't forget that bass."

Chapter VII

A couple of days later, Jack woke up with his usual well-deserved hangover. His effort to quietly slip out of Little Bohemia so as not to awaken the stranger lying upstairs in his bed was thwarted by one of his housemates, Dirty Ernie. Dirty Ernie stood at the top of the stairs and pulled his pants down just as Jack reached the front door below. "Hey, man. Would you take a look at this carbuncle? I think Kim gave me something."

Jack shook his head and sighed. "I'm not gonna look at that monster, Ernie." He was in no mood to give a medical opinion.

"Well, if you're headin' out pick up a couple six packs! We'll pay you back later!"

Jack heard a shuffling noise upstairs from the hallway where his bedroom was located across from Dirty Ernie's room. His overnight guest had been awakened from her sleep by Dirty Ernie and was now looking for Jack.

Jack had met this mysterious woman the previous night while working at a club downtown. The guitar player that night was a tall, handsome cockhound named Archie Clark, who had arrived in town just a few months before. Archie had introduced his comely friend to Jack and had taken it upon himself to convince Jack to let her stay with him for a couple of days while she was in town to attend her sister's funeral.

Jack was somewhat surprised when Archie floated this proposition by him because Archie never passed up a chance for a sexual encounter with a white woman. Jack later found out that she and Archie were just good friends from Baltimore and that Archie was shacked up with someone already. Someone who would not appreciate having a nymphomaniac named Kelly Sorenson around.

Kelly Sorenson was a slim brunette with big brown eyes and a button nose. She was on the lam from the law over some serious matters that involved the federal government and was desperate to lay low. Jack did not care to know anything beyond that. The previous night's sexual indulgences were enough to keep his mind and body occupied enough.

There were only two things Jack could remember about the previous night of revelry. Dirty Ernie's mutt, Dutch, had entered Jack's bedroom while he was performing coitus doggy-style with Kelly on his fold-out couch. The dog watched them intently with his tongue hanging out, panting away. As Jack made eye contact with Dutch, he couldn't help but think of the irony in that moment.

The only other instance he could recall was when Kelly, who was quite drunk and tripping on acid, decided to call the famous beat writer Charles Bukowski from the phone on Jack's night stand. She handed the phone to Jack, who immediately realized that he was unprepared for the moment and that Bukowski was obviously not interested in talking to a shit heel like him.

Now, standing next to Dirty Ernie and his exposed member, Kelly beckoned to Jack from the top of the stairs. "Baby doll, where ya think you're goin', huh?"

"Back to bed, baby. Back to bed," was all Jack could mutter.

Chapter VIII

It was a very hot day as Jack hoofed it down High St. to visit one of America's premier dive bars, Chet's Place. Dirty Ernie occasionally played there with his ill-rehearsed band of miscreants. They let him play because he was a regular who dropped a lot of coin there. The guy could drink and it was close to home.

Chet's was just across the street from Stax's, on the main drag just north of campus. Stax's was Jack's favorite place to hang out. It was where he had his first conversation with Willie, and where he was now playing most often due to the generosity of the club's owner, Sally.

Sally was the only club owner in town who genuinely appreciated the local musicians. She would often find a night or two during a slow week for Jack to play there with whatever musical line-up he could conjure up. Always happy to offer her stage to Jack, Sally gave him carte blanche to indulge himself with his various projects, which sometimes strayed into the avant-garde.

Jack figured that he'd kill some time with a couple cold ones at Chet's. Stax's would open when the sun went down. He paid for two beers at the bar and found a table in the corner of the room that was shielded from the sun, which was now low in the sky. He noticed his phone number had been carved into the wooden table. Likely the work of Dirty Ernie and his knife, or his drinking partner and lover, Kim. "For a good time, call…"

Jack drank the two perspiring bottles of Budweiser quickly in succession and soon his hangover was gone.

Noticing through the front window that the sign was now lit at Stax's, Jack headed across the street to see what might be on tap for the evening.

He stopped in the middle of High St. It was the strange time of day, just before dusk, when a person feels a peculiar melancholy. Jack paused for a moment to discover that there was very little activity taking place in the usually bustling neighborhood.

His spirits were revived when he saw Leon, the affable giant who dwarfed the stool, he was perched on just inside the door of Stax's. Leon was a serviceable bass player himself and an effective bouncer who knew how to get people to cooperate by his sheer size.

"Hey Leon, it says on the marquee that Lonnie Mack is here tonight. Really?"

"Yeah, really." Leon took Jack's fiver.

Jack had not heard the name Lonnie Mack for years. He even thought that he might have been dead. Lonnie Mack was one of the first heroes of the electric guitar in the early '60s. He had an instrumental hit, Memphis, which had put him on the map until the British Invasion became all the rage in America. Nevertheless, Mack had been a major influence to most of those guitar players from across the pond, such as Jeff Beck, Jimmy Page and Eric Clapton to name a few. Now he was hitting the roadhouse circuit years later.

Jack walked inside and spied Sally working solo behind the bar. As she brought Jack his customary bottle of Budweiser (there was a bottling plant a couple miles away and Bud was the beer of choice for the local beer drinking crowd), he couldn't help noticing that he was the only person in the joint. The entire room was empty except for five guys sitting down at the end of the bar.

"Where's everyone at? I know it's still early but it's Lonnie Mack tonight, right?"

"Those guys at the end of the bar are the band," Sally replied.

Jack did a double-take and sure enough he spied the stout, bearded fellow in the cowboy hat. Lonnie Mack. His Flying V guitar was onstage, leaning against his amp.

"Shit, buy those guys a round on me, and tell 'em they don't have to get up and play on my account. Let some more people get here first so it won't be so awkward."

She took them their drinks and they warmly displayed their appreciation by lifting their beers in Jack's direction before swilling them down.

"Damn," Jack muttered to himself. He knew the unpleasurable feeling that comes from performing for small or indifferent audiences and it's no fun. First you get to feeling sorry for yourself, and then you get to feeling sorry for the club owner until you get to feeling sorry for yourself again because the club owner is liable to blame you for the poor turnout and stiff you at the end of the night. That would not be the case tonight, however, because it was Sally's place.

Jack sat there with the profound feeling of, *If a tree falls in the woods and no one is around to hear it, does it make a sound*?

More time passed, and eventually the great man and his band ascended the steps leading to the stage and played. Jack was receiving a private concert from an inarguable legend and yet never had he felt so shitty. Well, at least the band was getting in a paid rehearsal.

In order to perform live there has to be some semblance of human interaction involving an audience. Otherwise, what's the point?

Jack clapped loudly and let out yelps of appreciation after each song, but it didn't help the situation much.

Wednesday nights can be murder. Even at Stax's.

Chapter IX

It was now Tropicana time, and Jack was going to play with his new friend Willie for the first time on a sweltering Saturday night. A small club, it was a tidy place operated by a tall, stately black woman named Mickey. It was sectioned off by a wall that separated the bar from the lounge area where the band played.

Jack noticed that the bandstand was against the wall that faced the street outside, and he was relieved to see that there was no window on that wall where someone could take a potshot at him from behind. Jack had learned to look for these types of nuances, including where the exits were located. He was starting to lose the desire of being harmed in a blues club. The music was becoming more of a priority now.

The band that Willie had assembled this night featured a gentleman named Blind John on organ and a new fellow who had just hit town from Georgia, Del Bloom. Del was a short, stubby, white redneck who initially seemed somewhat well-behaved and a bit shy. He let his guitar do all the talking.

After hearing this guy play just a few notes on his 1961 Gibson SG/Les Paul, the audience was in the palm of his hand. He proceeded to burn the room down with his raw, chilling tone and incredible blues chops that seemed to come from somewhere deep down south.

Jack cornered Del after the first set, before Del's new fans could descend on him to offer him drinks. "Where did you come from and how did you learn to play like that?"

Del said, "Well man, I used to hang out with the Allman Brothers Band when they first got together in Florida. Duane Allman showed me how to play the slide guitar and he'd let me sit in with 'em when I was still in high school. They were just starting to get noticed before they moved to Macon. The other guys didn't dig it when I'd sit in, but Duane took a liking to me and would sometimes slip me money because I was always followin' 'em around."

The Allman Brothers Band was the most influential southern-rock band of all time. Duane Allman was one of the guitar gods of rock music history, his legacy having grown ever since he was killed in a motorcycle accident in Macon, Georgia while in his prime. He had been a contributor with Eric Clapton on the iconic album Layla, by Derek and the Domino's.

"That guitar I'm playin' belonged to Duane. He used it on all his slide stuff."

Jack stared at Del and then asked, "You mean to tell me that the guitar you're playing tonight was the one used on the song Layla?"

"Yeah, it was," Del shot back.

"Duane had a premonition right before he got killed. He told his brother Gregg that if anything happened to him, he wanted me to have his guitar. They were gonna bury it with him, but Gregg made sure that I got it instead."

Jack could not help but be convinced. After having heard Del play during the previous set, it did appear that he was indeed for real. No sense disputing anything at this point.

As Del's admirers streamed toward them from the bar he told Jack, "Now I'm kinda in-between thangs and I been shacked up with a coupla whores and their pimp over on the south side."

While returning to the stage for the second set, the band discovered that they were now without a drummer. Brother Leroy Ellis had been scooped up by the police for buying drugs from an undercover officer between sets.

Jack volunteered to play Leroy's drums and Willie assumed the bass playing chores. As a young man, he had cut his teeth in Chicago as a bassist for virtually all the legends of modern urban blues. Now it was more of a chore, because he was a known entity for his blues crooning. To have to accompany himself was considered somewhat beneath him. That was the job of a sideman.

It would not have mattered who was playing the drums during that set. Del's sudden change of behavior resulted in an ear-splitting volume that negated any of the band's efforts to be heard above his din. Willie was doing a slow burn and Jack could sense that things were going down the tubes and fast. The drinks that Del had been plied with by his adoring fans had taken their toll on him. It was now evident that there were two Del's. Good Del and very bad Del.

Someone mercifully stuck a couple of quarters in the jukebox. Jack slinked away from the drum kit and slid unobtrusively onto the stool at the end of the bar. From triumph to tragedy in one set.

Before he could order, Mavis the bartender had some information for him. She put her heavily lipsticked mouth to his ears and whispered, "Creole's got it in for you tonight. Take a look around the corner, table at the back." Jack winced. That sounded bad. Turned out it wasn't bad. It was Cleo.

Jack peeked around the corner of the partition wall and there sat one of the call girls Del was living with. She was out for kicks tonight and she was indeed high class. Thin, with fashionably short dark hair and dark eyes that spelled danger. A creole beauty with flawless olive colored skin.

Jack walked back to the bar and found his drink waiting for him, as well as a phone number. "That's Cleo's number. She must be curious who's the white boy crazy enough to be playin' here." Cleo was a third-generation prostitute who was in demand by some of the biggest names in show business. One phone call was all it would take for her to be whisked off for a high-paying party with the Stones in L.A.

The third set never happened. Willie drifted off, having grown disinterested with the idea of having to play bass again, and Blind John somehow got himself locked in the men's room. The jukebox played on and Jack kept feeding it quarters until he could figure out what to do.

When Willie slipped out of the Tropicana, Jack had a feeling that Willie had checked out for the night. Probably heading to a clandestine house party nearby, usually in someone's basement with a makeshift bar, Willie always made the party swing. He was the guest of honor every place he went and he never felt guilty about not finishing out a night at a club.

Jack reached into his pocket for his last quarter when Cleo appeared before him in a strapless pink dress that accentuated her perfect body.

"Hey, did you get my number from Mavis? Do you need someone to help carry your stuff tonight? Del passed out and Mavis told me he could stay here tonight and sleep it off. I need a ride. I'll help you with whatever you want..."

Jack looked heavenward, and when he said, "Yeah, thanks," he knew at that moment that there had to be a God.

Chapter X

It was Jack's day off and he had Little Bohemia all to himself. The bums had cleared out of the house for the day and were off doing their thing. The doorbell rang and Jack opened the door to find his music addicted friend, Steve standing outside with a large grin on his face. Steve was a puffy looking fellow with short arms that barely hung to his waist. He sported a bowl haircut. He would rather spend his money on a few more albums for his immense music collection than pay for a haircut.

"King Crimson's at the Agora tonight, ya wanna go?"

Jack said, "Sounds good to me. Belew's in the band now with Fripp."

Steve reached into his pants pocket and produced some mushroom caps in a plastic bag.

"Let's eat these and then I'll come back tonight with the tickets." He handed Jack a few of the mushrooms and then promptly ate the rest as Jack went to the refrigerator for a couple of beers which would be required in order to wash away the nasty tasting psychedelics.

As Jack walked back into the living room, Steve had already regurgitated his share into his cupped hands and was contemplating his situation. Quickly, with a horrible look of resignation on his face, he forced his hands to his mouth and gulped the vomit back down into his pie-hole.

He accepted his beer with immense gratitude and paused between swallows just long enough to say, "Thanks, Jack. Johnny-On-The-Spot."

Jack ingested his mushrooms by gulping them down simultaneously with a large swig of beer. After a minute of nausea, he realized that he'd be OK.

Steve wiped his hands on his torn King Crimson T shirt and headed toward the door. "See ya later pal, this should be a good one tonight."

An hour later the mushrooms were taking effect. Jack was studiously exploring the palm of his hand in order to unlock the secrets of the universe. The doorbell rang again and Jack jumped. He hadn't been expecting more visitors.

This visitor was a small, thin, proudly indignant Puerto Rican woman named Sylvia. She was Bud Dixon's wife. For now.

She had an abnormally large rack for a woman of her slight build. She also had the ability to spit as casually as a man while walking down the street, puffing on a cigarette.

She couldn't help but put the needle to Jack. "Whatsa matter, clownface? You don't look so good." Sylvia disliked Jack because she didn't like sharing her husband with anyone, and Bud and Jack were now playing together more often with Big Art's New Nude Sex Revue.

"Listen Sylvia, I feel like a million bucks."

"Yeah, a million bucks in somebody else's pocket," she shot back. With that, she turned and abruptly walked out of the living room, giving Jack the finger on her way out. What a sweetheart. Jack knew it was only a matter of time before she and Bud would be through. Then it would be his turn to offer his old friend Bud a couch to sleep on. Bud would no doubt decline because he knew the history of that couch and Big Art.

A short time later in the afternoon, Jack would be interrupted by the doorbell yet again.

It was Del and his guitar. Jack had no idea how Del had found out where he lived. Paranoia from the acid trip was now kicking in.

"Hey Jack, I got somethin' for ya to hear, man." It was a cassette tape of a recording session that Del had recently done in England with guitarist Mick Taylor of the Rolling Stones.

Jack sat in a chair, fiddling with Del's Duane Allman guitar while Del pressed the play button and unsuspectingly sat on the couch of shame. "Can you tell which one's him and which one's me? I'm the one in the left speaker."

"Yeah, yeah," Jack said as he continued his assault on Del's guitar. He couldn't tell the difference between the two because of the poor recording quality of the tape and the fact that he was now tripping.

Chapter XI

Afternoon turned to evening as Steve appeared with the tickets to the concert. Del had left hours earlier. Jack and Steve were both still flying high on the mushrooms and were in a more comfortable mental state than they had been in earlier that afternoon. Now Jack was experiencing the enhanced awareness of the minutia of life, that his mind would not ordinarily take notice of.

With addled bemusement, they made the short walk to campus and entered into the fray of rock fans who had already crammed into the Agora. Within minutes they had somehow slinked their way through the throng and found themselves standing front and center on the main floor in front of the stage, physically being pressed up against the stage by the rowdy crowd. This was to be an important event. A supergroup was going to be debuting material from their new album.

Jack noticed that front man Adrian Belew's assortment of guitar distortion pedals were onstage within arm's reach of him. He could reach out and toggle Belew's wah-wah pedal if he wanted to. Steve used his girth to create a little space for them to breathe.

The stage lights went up and Jack found that Belew was now standing over him as the crowd went wild with the anticipation of a killer show. There was one problem, however. Someone must have failed to check the stage monitors.

King Crimson were using new electronic technology with regard to their instruments. Even the drums were electronic. Without monitors, no one in the band could hear each other, and this created an insurmountable obstacle for them.

Jack had heard their new album and was familiar with the band's material. He immediately realized that something was wrong as soon as they started playing because the new music being presented was not synchronized, which was a major part of what made the complexity of their music intriguing.

Jack could not contain himself, bursting out in laughter at the band and their predicament. The arrogant sons-of-bitches had outsmarted themselves by becoming wholly reliant on their newfound technology and it was failing them miserably. Belew looked over his shoulder in bewilderment at the band's founder and other guitarist, Robert Fripp. Fripp was perched on his little stool, as was his custom, furiously attempting to give the international signal for "Cut" by making a slashing motion across his bow-tied neck.

Jack realized the audience was too worked up with excitement to notice that what they were hearing was an abject mess. The song fell apart, and the faithful fans had no idea that what they had just witnessed was an aborted effort, so they actually cheered.

At that moment Jack noticed that all four members of King Crimson were staring directly at him. They could not ignore him because it was obvious that he was the only person there who knew what was happening and they hated him for it.

As the stagehands rushed furiously about the stage, Fripp could only sit there, glaring at Jack with his beady eyes. Belew looked directly down at Jack, mouthing, "You little piss ant."

Chapter XII

Jack had more than a bit of trepidation as he lugged his equipment from the parking lot, heading across the street to The Stop-On-In on Mt. Vernon Ave. It was a humid, gray evening and he wasn't looking forward to what would be a rowdy Saturday crowd. He sensed an ominous vibe hanging in the air.

There had been more than a fair share of violent activity in and around the neighborhood recently. Jack was only playing this gig because Willie had asked him. It was an important night for Willie because many of his friends from the steel mill would be there and he wanted to give them a good show. Del was still with the band, and his behavior had become even more erratic and alcohol-fueled recently. Yet, that wasn't the most worrisome thing on Jack's mind as he made his way to the sidewalk in front of The Stop-On-In.

Ten people had been murdered in a Chinese restaurant only a block away the previous weekend. Word on the street was that it was a professional job perpetrated by a gang war between factions of the local tong. That same night a 17-year-old girl had been raped and strangled in the lot where Jack had just parked, and the next night an elderly man had been robbed of his social security check and was shot in the head just a few feet from where Jack's Volvo wagon now sat. The bloodstains in the gravel were an affirmation of that.

This was a night when it didn't feel so sexy to get whacked. That sick, romantic notion had faded from Jack's psyche long ago. He just wanted to play this gig and get out of there alive.

He pushed his amplifier toward the front door, which was held open by a brick and a microphone stand. There was already a lot of commotion taking place inside the darkened bar as he stepped inside. Before he could adjust his eyes, he felt a sharp, stinging pain across the back of his neck. A small dark man had stealthily emerged from the sidewalk behind Jack and had struck him with a two-by-four.

Immediately, an elderly man leapt off his stool behind the bar and rushed to the doorway, placing the business end of a .38 caliber revolver in the attacker's mouth, backing him against the wall of the bar outside the doorway. "Don't you go messin' with my musicians, you cocksucker!" That threat came from the small, elderly black owner of The Stop-On-In, Earl Monroe. "Drop that motherfuckin' stick, boy!" Earl had to have been eighty years old, yet he was amazingly spry. He plunged the barrel of the pistol deeper into the mouth of the man. "Don't let me ever see your dumb fuckin' ass around here again!"

Standing there on the sidewalk, Jack noticed Earl's son-in-law, Nate. Nate was ready to pounce, but he didn't want to get in the way, since it appeared that Earl had things under control and maybe was having a little fun showing off for Jack.

Nate stood there, looking like John Shaft, one handsome slick dude. He was definitely a guy who could take care of himself. He would have likely been the heir apparent to the Stop-On-In if he hadn't gotten killed in a motorcycle accident, impaled on a utility pole a block away.

The man dropped the board and Earl yelled, "Now git!" The fellow sprinted quickly down the sidewalk as Earl retrieved the board and slung it at him. They watched it rotate wildly through the thick evening air in a perfect arc, striking Jack's attacker on the back of the head, knocking him to the ground. "That'll teach 'em to go fuckin' with my musicians."

Once inside the bar, Jack realized what the excitement was about. There was going to be a heavyweight title fight that night featuring the undefeated great black champ, Larry Holmes and a mismatched, brawling redneck named Randall "Tex" Cobb. It was to be broadcast on the small black and white television that was perched on a shelf above the bar.

This is going to be a bloodbath, thought Jack. A mismatch of epic proportion, Cobb had no chance of winning the fight. This was to be fifteen rounds of torture featuring a white stiff who was too tough to get knocked out getting unmercifully pummeled by the champ. *Shit,* Jack thought, *Impeccable timing.* Jack and Del would be the only two white faces in the bar that evening.

Chapter XIII

The band kicked off the first set just as the fighters were making their ring entrances. As usual, Willie had told the band to warm up the audience by playing a couple instrumentals until he felt it was the proper time to be introduced.

Del turned to the band before the first song and said, "Let's change things up tonight. I'm gonna sing a few first."

Noting that Del had already been hitting the Wild Turkey hard, which always got him in trouble, Jack tried to reason with him, "I don't think that would be very wise of you, Del. This crowd isn't in any mood for that tonight and Willie will definitely get pissed off if the band doesn't come off sounding good. It's his crowd tonight."

Willie's buddies from the mill had been promised a special show featuring the hottest new guitar player in town. Now they would be in for something different.

After singing a couple sloppy versions of some Howlin' Wolf tunes, Del got the bright idea to serenade the already unimpressed and confused audience with an instrumental he had written, inspired by his days of playing southern rock music. It was definitely the wrong time and place for that.

Jack could hear the scuffling of feet and shifting of tables in the awkward silence after the song. Del was met with catcalls of, "Play us some real shit, white boy!" and "Don't be bringin' that cracker ass shit 'round here, you stupid motherfucker!" Jack heard the bell signaling the end of the sixth round coming from the bar.

There was a cry of pain from the restroom in the back. Nate later told Jack that, "It was nothin', just a guy settlin' a gambling debt with a blade."

Willie was now onstage, decked out in pink and trying to revive the crowd and salvage the night. He exhorted the room to, "Drink up, get drunk, get to be somebody!"

An angry old hag yelled back, "I am somebody, fool. You think we all ain't somebody?"

A roar erupted from the bar. The champ had Cobb on the ropes and was toying with his prey, having already knocked him down three times and opening a large gash over Cobb's left eye. Maybe the ref would mercifully stop the fight on cuts. A TKO would have been a godsend. But Cobb was too tough to quit, a game fighter who had a good cut man in his corner that night.

There was a rising tide of hatred building in the room. A mob was assembling at the bar, growing with each passing round.

Chapter XIV

Back onstage, Del was becoming a mean drunk. Jack saw the kind of meanness that only Wild Turkey could conjure in an alcoholic. Willie looked at Jack with those wet and bulging eyes as if to ask, "Can't you do something about Del?"

Jack shrugged his shoulders and spoke softly, "Too late, Will. Too late."

Another roar from the bar brought a shudder to Jack. Cobb must be in trouble again, too.

Jack wondered for a moment if it might be possible for Willie to take him along on one of his late-night excursions to a house party. Like right now. They could leave and not come back. Maybe no one would notice because everyone was watching the fight.

Jack would have no such luck on this night.

It was around the tenth round when Jack heard the gunshot. He actually felt it as it whizzed past his leg in the middle of Sweet Home Chicago. Instinctively, he jumped off the stage and dove for cover under the nearest pool table. He stayed huddled under there, watching the masses of legs moving wildly back and forth in panic. Then he saw a pair of pink trousers stop in front of him.

Willie poked his head under the table and gave Jack a hard look, saying in mock disgust, "Get on up outta there. A man would rather walk through hell in a pair of gasoline britches than mess with you while I'm around." His assurance did nothing to convince Jack that no harm would befall him if he left his safe haven at that moment. "No way, man. I'm staying put."

After some time, things began to simmer down a bit. Jack still stayed put until a pair of spindly bare legs appeared before him. A comely little buck-toothed girl peeked under the table and said, "Hi. My name's Sunshine. I'm fo'teen years old and I can turn you inside out." She was obviously unfazed by the warfare that had just taken place and was intent on turning a trick.

Jack emerged from his hiding place because he had been brought to shame by Sunshine. If she could ignore the danger in order to do some business, then Jack felt obliged to return to his place alongside Willie on the bullet-riddled stage.

The Holmes/Cobb fight lasted the entire fifteen rounds as Jack had predicted. It was also the bloodbath that Jack had predicted. The crowd watching the fight had been incited to the viciousness that Jack had predicted. Jack should have been playing a roulette wheel in Vegas that night instead of playing The Stop-On-In. Jack could have even predicted what was to come next, but would not have been able to stop it.

Willie approached Jack after the last set as he was beginning to gather his gear. The music was over, a fifteen-round affair in itself.

"Here, dude. Earl paid up and here's your cut." Willie smiled as he paid Jack, and it was obvious that he had a bit too much alcohol himself during the night.

"Thanks, Will. See you on the flip-flop."

A few minutes later, Jack was exiting the men's room and was approached by Willie again. "Here ya go, man. A good night's work." Again, he thrust money into Jack's hand. Jack had never been paid twice for the same gig before, but he was too tired to give it any thought. He was ready to go home.

Chapter XV

Jack was Del's ride for the night and the night was now over. Everything was loaded and locked into Jack's car. Everything except Del.

Jack walked back into The Stop-On-In to collect Del, and upon entering, he heard Del's voice screaming from the back of the bar. "Listen here, Willie, you think I'm a god damn nigger or something? A white nigger, huh? Well fuck you, you black bastard!" Del was just getting started. "You better pay me, motherfucker!"

Willie was keeping his composure despite being verbally abused in the company of his friends and the other bar patrons, who were now eyeing him with curiosity, wondering just how much more he could take. Del was challenging Willie for his money and was using fighting words for everyone to hear.

It hadn't yet dawned on Jack that Willie had paid him twice because Willie had mistakenly thought that Jack was Del on one of the occasions. They were the only two white guys in the band, and Willie had become confused by being more drunk than usual due to the generosity of his friends that night.

Jack was quickly heading for the exit, yelling over his shoulder to Del, "Last call, asshole. I'm outta here. You better move it if you want a ride!"

As Jack crossed Mt. Vernon Ave., he could still hear the "N" bombs coming from inside the bar, and by the time he reached his car, he finally saw Del emerge onto the sidewalk outside. Starting the Volvo, Jack thrust the passenger door open and revved the engine, imploring Del to hurry the hell up.

Del almost made it across the street before he turned and headed back in the direction of the bar. Willie had just emerged with his friends and Del was stalking toward him, continuing to drop the "N" bombs. Jack slammed the door shut and yelled out, "You're on your own now, dumbass!" He paused just long enough to see Willie and Del converge in the middle of the street.

Willie often carried a briefcase with him to gigs and it usually contained nothing. It was just part of a blues man's ensemble, an accessory to add a bit of hubris to the attire. It can also be used as a weapon, for Willie gave it one quick, mighty roundhouse of a swing that struck Del along the side of his head, dropping him to the pavement. A perfectly aimed blow. Del lay motionless in the street, and Jack winced as Willie gave Del's prone body a kick for good measure. Jack understood that he had no recourse but to kick Del's ass or risk losing face in front of his friends and the bar's patrons who were now spilling outside to watch the action.

Jack quickly exited the parking lot and didn't even bother unloading any equipment when he arrived home at Little Bohemia. It was 3:00 A.M. and he was spent.

At 5:30 A.M., his telephone woke him. It was Del. "Hey, pick me up, will ya?"

Groggily, Jack asked, "Where you at?"

Del answered as if nothing out of the ordinary had transpired that evening, "I'm back at the bar, havin' a drink with my new friends."

Angrily Jack responded, "Del, I never want to see you or hear from you again." And then he hung up.

Jack never did see or hear from Del again. Del came for his gear the next day when Jack wasn't home and that was that.

It was later, after having thought about the mix-up with the money which led to Del's tirade at The Stop-On-In that Jack began to feel partly responsible for Del getting his ass kicked.

Chapter XVI

He decided to make things right when he got a call from Del's old housemate, Cleo. She needed a ride from the airport, where she was returning from yet another high-paying rock and roll excursion as a human party favor.

Cleo had been calling Jack with more frequency recently, and even though it was always for a ride, he was beginning to get the feeling that there was something more to it than that. She trusted him and enjoyed his company because he had always displayed a casual, non-judgmental attitude toward her, and that made her feel comfortable when she was with him because he conveniently ignored her business. That is, he pretended to ignore her business.

She was slowly becoming the one woman who he actually looked forward to being with, even though those occasions were always initiated by her. He had yet to call her when he found himself longing for her company, fearing that it would send her a signal that could possibly scare her away from him.

After picking her up at the airport, they would usually stop off somewhere for a couple of drinks and often end their night in his bed.

"Listen, Cleo. Give this money to Del when you see him." Jack had even included his own cut from that evening so Del could get double pay.

"I'll give Del the money if I see him 'cause I'm sure he's gonna need it. He got bounced out of the house before I left."

Jack ran into Willie at Chet's Place a couple evenings later and told Willie that he'd made things right with Del and was sorry to have played a part in the confusion at The Stop-On-In on Saturday.

Willie pulled a handkerchief from his coat pocket, dabbing at his eyes. "Shit, man. I felt bad about the way things went down, myself. I paid the sucker twice too! Well, it looks like Del got paid four times for a proper ass whuppin'."

Months later, Jack was in a music store, killing time while waiting for someone to fix some damage to his bass. He idly flipped through one of the guitar magazines that always seem to be laying around those shops. Some of those rags had a fold-out section in the middle, a la Playboy. Upon folding out this particular magazine's three-piece section, he realized that he was looking at a photograph of Del's guitar, the 1961 Gibson SG/Les Paul.

There was an accompanying story of the guitar's provenance and how Duane Allman's premonition had led to Del's having come into its possession, confirmed verbatim by Gregg Allman.

"I'll be damned," Jack whispered to no one in particular.

The article went on to note that the guitar had recently been sold at auction. The guitar fetched $591,000, making it one of the twenty most expensive guitars in existence.

Jack couldn't help but chuckle at the memory of having played that guitar on a lazy afternoon in Little Bohemia while tripping on mushrooms.

Chapter XVII

Jack Bradley and Marcus Brown and a night on the town. No work tonight and an invite from Sally to see both shows of the great Jaco Pastorius at Stax's. Jack had really ingratiated himself with that club since hitting town, and now he and his drummer were in for a special night. How special, they never could have guessed.

Pastorius was the greatest electric bass player in the world, with no one surpassing him since his death, which would come soon enough after this night. Jack had always appreciated Pastorius as an innovative genius, but he hadn't yet heard the rumblings going around about the demons tormenting the alcohol- and cocaine-fueled bi-polar nut.

As was often the case at that time when someone's star had fallen a bit, as with Lonnie Mack, Pastorius was making the rounds of college towns. Travelling in a van with his trio and his girlfriend, picking up gigs along the way based on his name, he was in a bad way. The band was barnstorming with the sole intention of supporting Jaco's habit as he was sliding into the abyss that would eventually claim him.

The abuse he heaped on the audience of admiring fans at Stax's was well beyond what Jack had heard from Neal Ledbetter at My Sister's Place. Columbus was often referred to as "Cowtown," and Pastorius must have been told this because he used it to remind the audience between songs what hicks they were. Nonetheless, he survived because he was the greatest bass player in the world when he was on his game, which he wasn't on this night.

Jack and Marcus were allowed to stay in the club while the room was being cleared for the second show and Pastorius had noted this when he emerged from backstage to fetch something from behind his amplifier, no doubt wondering who the two dudes were, standing at the bar chatting it up with Sally. He shot a quick stink eye in their direction and retreated backstage again.

"So, what do you fellas think?" Sally really wanted their opinion.

"Well, Sally, he's pretty wasted and I think he's feelin' kinda raunchy tonight. I don't know if he can do another show without embarrassing someone, hopefully not you." Marcus looked at the ground, studying the patterns on the worn carpet forlornly.

"He's a cocky motherfucker tonight," chimed in Jack. "We'll see."

Sally looked sullen. "At forty bucks a pop for a forty-five-minute set..." She was thinking about her paying audience, not wanting them to be let down. The place was going to be packed for both shows, yet she would have rather taken a loss at the door than have a bad show at Stax's. Too late now.

Jack hoped that the next set would be a boisterous one from the zealous road warrior, eager to please the audience with a display of musical abandon. The trio was now warmed up after the first show and came out smoking.

However, midway during the second show, after playing a strange rendition of *Ode To Billie Joe* and a very loosely improvised Jimi Hendrix mash-up, Jaco returned to his Neal Ledbetter mode and started in again with the insults. The audience initially thought it must be part of his act. However, their wariness soon came to the fore as he began to heckle them mercilessly. "You fuckin' hicks wouldn't know good music if it was jammed up yer ass!"

Spying a recognizable face in the audience, Jaco brightened for a moment, a slight glow of humanity alighting upon his face for a split second. "Hey, Ralph! Ralph's in the house, everybody. Ralph is one badass dude! Shit, yeah." Ralph was a fellow bassist with a fair degree of recognition, having played with Ray Charles for years. "You hillbillies wouldn't know that. You don't know shit from nothin', assholes."

Jack felt a spookiness creep over him. He was witnessing a hard-core meltdown of a musical genius on display before a crowd of once adoring fans. It reminded him that every performance has a story behind it which the audience is rarely privy to.

The set mercifully came to an end, but not before Jaco spied an idle electric piano that was inexplicably sitting by its lonesome in a darkened corner at the rear of the stage. As his bandmates made their exit from the stage, he sat down and serenaded the remainder of the crowd with a sloppy improvisation of one of his compositional masterpieces, *Three Views Of A Secret*. Jack saw it as a rare glimpse of the fine line that separates genius from madness.

Sometimes there is a price to be paid when it comes to having achieved artistic greatness, and at that moment Jack was thankful that he himself wasn't so great.

The room had completely cleared again, and the night that was once filled with promise had left Sally, Jack and Marcus feeling deflated. As was the case after the first show, they were the only three people remaining in the club.

"Well, that was…something," Sally remarked as she poured the boys one last one for the road. They were standing at the bar where they had been camped out all night when Jaco reappeared with his bandmates and his girlfriend, who appeared agitated and in a hurry to get a move on.

Jaco noticed the interlopers and decided to approach Marcus. "Hey, fucker! Whatcha think you're doin' hittin' on my wife? I oughta kick your fuckin' ass, you little shit!"

Jack couldn't help but think of the irony of that moment. Although slight of build, Marcus would have been much more than Jaco had bargained for. As chance would have it, he had just been awarded his black belt in karate that afternoon. Jack stood by to see what would happen, ready to intervene.

Marcus was unusually calm. "Jaco, you got it all wrong. I love you, man. I would never…" He was suddenly interrupted by Jaco's woman, who had hastily made her way across the room after having obviously witnessed similar scenes with regularity during her time on the road, on the bum with the king of punk jazz.

"Goddamn it, Jaco, I'm not your wife! Quit telling people that I'm your fucking wife! Leave this fucking guy alone! Let's get the hell out of this hole. Now!"

Jack was now pissed. Her insult had hurt Sally, who had been standing just across from them behind the bar. It showed on her face. She didn't deserve that.

Jaco retreated to the stage to load the last of his gear, and Jack got more than a small bit of satisfaction from seeing that the great man had no money to pay a roadie to do his heavy lifting for him as he was accustomed to during his glory days.

The fellows bade their patron, Sally, adieu and made their way to Marcus' for a nightcap. Upon arriving, Jack flicked on the TV and began channel surfing while sipping at his beer. Marcus was in the kitchen making a pizza when there was a knock at the door. It was 2:30 A.M.

Fletch called out with some legitimate concern, "Who's there?" His concern arose from the fact that he was one of the most active cocaine dealers in town. A lot of musicians were users and many of them had a side hustle like Marcus.

"It's me, Rick." Rick Ellis was a saxophone player who was just starting to make the scene in Cowtown. Marcus let him in and Rick chose to stand just inside the doorway. He was a big lug, with horn-rimmed glasses and long sideburns. "Hey, there's a party over at Ralph's and Jaco's there. Ralph said that you guys are invited if you wanna come over." Jack and Marcus gave each other a quick glance.

"I'm in the middle of making some food and I think I'll take a pass. I don't think Jack's up for it, either."

"Well…do you have any blow I could score? It's Jaco for cryin' out loud Are you sure you guys don't wanna pass this up?"

"Nah, but I'll hook you up. Just wait a minute. Pizza won't be ready for another ten minutes. How much you want?"

"Three grams'll do."

Marcus disappeared into the bathroom. Jack wasn't a user, but he knew what Marcus was up to. He could hear the razor blade chopping furiously on the countertop in the john. Marcus was no doubt preparing a treat for Rick to deliver to the party guests. Cocaine laced with baby laxative and a couple other nasty additives that would make a dog puke and shit for days.

"Here ya go, Rick. That'll be three bills."

Rick paid up and was gone. Within minutes, he arrived at Ralph's apartment. Jaco was there with Ralph and three others, including Jaco's "wife." Rick made it a party of six. He flashed a smile at the group who were lounging in Ralph's living room, giving them a wink as he made his way into Ralph's lavatory. They were listening to some of Jaco's records from Ralph's collection as Jaco was holding court.

Rick meticulously took a credit card from his wallet and laid out six perfect lines of cocaine on a mirror that he found lying next to the sink. Then, with some aplomb he made his way to the living room and handed the mirror to Jaco. Big mistake. Jaco rapidly did all six lines in succession and handed the mirror back to him. The rest of the group could only stare at Jaco. They were crestfallen, but what could they say to a superstar?

The rest of the night deteriorated rapidly, with Jaco insisting on playing all of his greatest hits on Ralph's turntable. Ralph bristled with anger every time Jaco grabbed the stylus and dragged the needle across Ralph's once pristine records whenever he wanted to hear a specific passage of music a second or third or tenth time.

By the time the sun had risen in the morning, Ralph felt a great relief when Jaco and his crew climbed into their van and headed off to Pittsburgh.

Chapter XVIII

The harsh tone of a ringing phone woke Jack from his slumber. This morning he found himself at Vivian's apartment. Vivian was a waifish little waitress who was considerably older than him who possessed prolific abilities in bed. Lately, he had been running a hot streak with the groupie scene and it was getting out of hand.

After his car died a week ago, he had found it convenient to use the services of whatever girl, he was with at the moment to give him a ride to his next destination after their business together was satisfied. Without fail, his partners would gladly drive him home, to a gig or even to the apartment of his next sexual encounter with no questions asked.

Jack wondered if it was possible that a secret league of women existed who had created an intelligence network designed to identify men who could give them physical satisfaction. It appeared to him that women were now approaching him with such a frequency for physical activity that it had to be attributed to more than word of mouth because none of these women knew each other, and they were now only growing in number. He had never experienced anything like this before, and even though he never felt that he was being used, he was starting to feel the shallowness of the act itself. One can only put so many notches in their bedpost before it becomes somewhat meaningless. Still, even meaningless sex was better than no sex to most young men.

Vivian called to him from her kitchen, "Jack, it's Dirty Ernie on the phone. He needs to ask you something important."

As Jack climbed from her bed, he suddenly felt spooked that he might be spending too much time with her at night.

The idea that she was falling in love with him was against the unspoken rule that was the basis for all of his liaisons. Until lately, she had maintained a laissez-faire attitude with regard to his one-off dalliances.

"I'm coming, Viv. What time is it?"

"It's time for you to talk to your friend. It's ten."

"How late were we up? I feel wiped out."

"We were up long enough. And I'm not done with you, so come out here and talk to your loser friend. I'll be back in bed."

Jack tried to get his legs back under him. They were weak, and as he walked to the bedroom door, he recalled having screwed Vivian at some point during the night while she was standing on her head.

Jack made it to the kitchen and took the phone that was dangling by its cord from her hand. She grabbed him and squeezed her naked body tightly against his, working her tongue into his mouth as she began to mount him standing up. The morning sun poured in through the window, illuminating her mussed-up hair as Jack ran his hands through it.

Jack was tempted to drop the phone and take her right there on the floor, not caring if Dirty Ernie was listening or not. This would surely make Vivian even more inspired to perform what came so naturally to her.

Chapter XIX

Jack picked the phone up from the kitchen floor and put it to his ear. The sound of a dial tone indicated that Dirty Ernie had hung up at some point over the past twenty minutes. He decided to call Little Bohemia from where he was lying in a puddle of perspiration on the dirty tile floor. As Vivian climbed off of him and began to stand up, she slipped and fell flat on her ass next to him. She rolled onto her side and propped herself up on one arm, watching Jack intently, now curious to find out what Dirty Ernie had called about.

"Ernie, sorry. The phone service here at Vivian's is lousy. What do you want?"

"Kim and I are getting married today. We're gonna do it in the living room with a preacher and everything. Do you have any suits that I can wear?"

"Well shit, Ern. I've got a couple of pinstripes in my closet. A blue one and a gray one. Take your pick and go ahead and keep whichever one fits you best."

"That's great, brother! You'll be there, won't you?" Dirty Ernie was on cloud nine. He and Kim had been shacked up across the hallway from Jack's room for a few years now. They were just a couple old barflies who considered Jack as something akin to a little brother. They didn't have much outside of each other and alcohol.

Jack asked, "So what time are the nuptials?"

"In an hour."

"I'll be there. I'll wear whatever suit you're not wearing. Damn, who's going to marry you guys?"

"Chet, he's an ordained minister. At least he said he was."

"Well, for as much money as you guys have spent in his joint over the years, he had better be doing this one on the house."

"He sure as hell is," Dirty Ernie said with some pride, "and he's even catering the party afterwards!"

"Does that mean he's bringing a keg, and some pickled eggs?" Jack chided him.

"How'd you know?" Dirty Ernie asked.

Jack chuckled. "Wow, I can't believe you're going to get married in an hour. I'll be there as soon as I can."

Vivian had now gotten to her feet and was standing at the sink, splashing water on her face. Jack could tell what was going through her mind. He had kept his private life separate from hers and he would not be inviting her to accompany him to the wedding. He stared at her for the longest time, waiting for her to turn around or say something, but she wouldn't. She knew the rules, and at this moment Jack felt the cruelty of what he had created not only for himself but for others.

"I'd better get going, Viv. You know I…"

"Shut up and go. I've got things to do today myself."

Jack knew that he could have her again that night if he wished.

Chapter XX

When Jack arrived home, he realized that Chet's Place had temporarily been closed in order to relocate a couple blocks north on High St. at Little Bohemia for the afternoon. All of the regular denizens of the dive bar were in his living room and were making themselves welcome. He recognized many of the characters who had already swooped down on the keg of beer that Chet had supplied as promised. The keg also appeared to serve as a makeshift pulpit for the ceremony.

Jack headed upstairs to change into whatever suit Dirty Ernie had chosen not to wear for his big day. It was close to go time and the keg was likely almost empty. Changing hastily into the blue suit that had been left hanging in his closet, Jack felt a sudden pang of guilt about not including Vivian. Today might have been the high point of her week, but it still wasn't worth the risk for Jack to let her get closer to him on an emotional level. He knew just enough about women by now to know that he would never be able to figure out the female animal, and he had played it safe so far. Even with Cleo, who was now starting to consume more of his thoughts with each passing day. It was becoming apparent to him that he was experiencing a kinship with a woman which extended beyond the physical realm, and it felt right.

Chet's unmistakably grating voice could now be heard barking from the living room. He was directing his drunken patrons to bring themselves to some semblance of order and they were not cooperating. Chet had a duty to perform, and he wanted to get on with it.

Jack hustled downstairs to the living room in time to see the bride and groom for the first time that day. Kim had gone out of her way to spruce herself up as best as possible and had likely sacrificed some of her drinking money in order to buy a new dress for the occasion. Dirty Ernie was in Jack's gray suit, which fit him reasonably well except for the fact that he couldn't button the jacket over his immense beer belly. The couple stood in the middle of the room, surrounded by their drinking buddies who were now making an attempt to exhibit some semblance of order. The keg had indeed become the pulpit, with Chet standing behind it with his Gideon bible placed atop it.

Standing at the bottom of the stairs, Jack watched Dirty Ernie's face intently. Things had happened so fast with this marriage business, yet this moment felt like it had some logic to it. Dirty Ernie's eyes would not lie and Jack studied them, curious to see for himself if he could recognize the look of love.

At that moment, there was nothing to see in those eyes except a sudden, drunken rage. Walking unsuspectingly through the front door into the midst of the sacred proceeding came Big Mike Stone, one of the former residents of Little Bohemia. He had arrived unannounced because he had not been invited. Big Mike Stone had the appearance of a cave man and had previously lived in the basement. A look of surprise crossed his bearded face.

"I hope I'm not interrupting anything; I just came to pick up my old softball bat that I forgot to take when I moved out."

Dirty Ernie had done a number on the keg since its arrival, and he was well-oiled. He rushed into the kitchen and returned with the softball bat that he had hidden behind the refrigerator.

Dirty Ernie had stumbled across his fiancé, and Big Mike Stone screwing on the couch of shame after Big Mike had moved out a month before, without them having seen him. Knowing that Big Mike was fond of his bat, Dirty Ernie had taken it upon himself to carve the name KIM into the bat and stash it from sight until the time was right for him to produce it and use Big Mike Stone's head for batting practice. The time was apparently now.

Waving the bat menacingly over his head he screamed, "I can't believe that you have the balls to be here, you rotten bastard! I saw you and Kim fucking! You fucked her on the goddamn couch! I thought that if she and I got married I could start to get over that, but now…"

Kim let out an awful howl. It was the sound of a woman who had seen hard times and was now considered damaged goods. This was just another terrible moment in her tumultuous life that, up until now, she had hoped was finally behind her.

The crowd of barflies that had once encircled Kim in the living room now panicked and rushed for the door. They would soon reconvene at Chet's Place to get the lowdown from Chet as to what had happened next. Chet would not be able to provide them with any details however, because he was the first one out the door.

Big Mike Stone backed against the wall; his eyes wide. Kim dropped to her knees, bursting out in tears as Dirty Ernie stood over her, taking practice swings with the bat.

"I'm so sorry! It was just one time and we were both drunk and you were playing with your band at Chet's and..."

"Shut the hell up, you wench!" Dirty Ernie looked ferocious. Jack looked at Dirty Ernie as if he were an animal, prepared to bludgeon someone to death. He was going to keep his damn mouth shut. Sometimes the peacekeeper ends up getting the worst of it. It looked like Big Mike Stone knew enough not to open his yap, either. It was now up to Dirty Ernie how this was going to play out.

"I love you, Ernie. I really, really do. Please forgive me. It was just one time and I don't know what made me do it. When I drink I don't think straight. You know how it is."

There was a long pause. "Yeah, I know." A tear ran down the side of Dirty Ernie's face as he turned toward Big Mike Stone. "Get out, now! I should kill you."

Big Mike Stone made a hasty exit. He was normally a tough guy and a brawler, but he left without his bat.

Dirty Ernie dropped the bat to the ground and walked out the front door. It would be days before he returned and no one ever asked him where he went.

When he did return, he and Kim arranged for a quick marriage at the courthouse downtown and went about their lives as they had before. Or so it appeared.

Chapter XXI

Jack was relaxing at home in Little Bohemia when the phone rang. He was killing time before heading out toward the airport to play with Willie at a dump called The Ambassador. Dirty Ernie called out from the kitchen, "Hey Jack, it sounds like your dad on the phone." Jack climbed up off the floor where he'd been reclining amidst a host of party-goers. He found the phone resting idly on the stove.

Jack grabbed the phone. "Hey, Dad, what's up?"

"Hey, Jack, how're you doing?" Before Jack could answer, his father continued, "You know, I think it's high time that you got your ass back here to Doveland and get real. You're wasting that degree of yours horsing around and I've got a job for you."

Jack figured that his degree in political science was a wasted degree even before he had graduated. He was in college to play baseball anyway, and when he blew out his elbow in his sophomore season, he was content just to be able to play for four years even though the pain was enormous. After he hurt his arm, he would never be able to throw hard again.

He was the only guy on the team who had graduated his senior year, even though he was rarely in class due to an overly ambitious schedule of games that were played on the road. Playing gigs in houses of ill-repute at night only created more of a disconnect with what one would consider a healthy student life experience.

When he was interviewed by the editor of an Akron newspaper because he had pitched a one hitter and somehow lost, he was quoted as saying, "I'll probably move to Columbus or Cincinnati soon to continue playing jazz." It made for a story in the sports pages because it is somewhat rare for a ballplayer to pursue interests as diverse as sports and music simultaneously. Upon reading his comment in the paper, Jack knew that he had backed himself into a corner and was obliged to move to one of those cities, lest he be considered a liar.

"Jack, are you still there? You're not saying anything. Listen, I just bought your aunt's house and you can move in rent-free until you get squared away. Sound good? Good. Your mom and I can't wait to have you back home. Frankly, we were starting to worry that you might fall in with that lifestyle and never get out. Now's the time to get real."

Jack offered no resistance because he suddenly realized how numb he had become, since he had allowed his life to repetitiously scuffle along. Timing is everything, and at that moment it went through his mind how many of his acquaintances had died recently. Neal Ledbetter had overdosed on heroin, found sitting upright in his chair, surrounded by his precious mineral collection, which was later returned to Ohio State. Marcus Brown had OD'd, too. Rick Ellis committed suicide and Del Bloom had accidently drowned.

Jack felt that it was now time to move on to whatever. Whatever was good enough, because he was still a young man, and he could always revert back to this life. He knew this life. That's why it was easy for him to say, "I'll be home in a week, Dad. Just want to take some time to get things in order. Thanks for everything and tell Mom I love her. See you in around a week."

Chapter XXII

Jack Bradley pulled his car into the parking lot of The Ambassador just as a massive jet was coming in for a landing. The roar of the engines in the darkness overhead gave him a quick thrill because the plane was coming in low. He grabbed his bass and headed for the front entrance to check out the scene.

When he entered the room, he realized that another band was already playing onstage. Sensing that there was an obvious mix-up because this kind of joint wouldn't hire two bands in one night, Jack looked around and saw Willie standing at the end of the bar. He was in a heated argument with the club's owner Milt Moore, a once famous jazz organist. Milt was now a washed-up curmudgeon, and he was infuriating Willie by intently played his pinball machine as if Willie wasn't there. Nobody likes the old cold shoulder, and this only intensified Willie's onslaught.

Jack stood by the front door to observe the one-sided discourse just as Willie's drummer for the night, Mo Styles appeared. "Man, sure looks like Willie's givin' it to Milt. What the hell's the deal?"

Jack answered, "Well, shit. It looks like Milt double-booked the night and the other band got here first. Now

Willie's probably trying to get some money for us, but it doesn't look like Milt is gonna budge."

"I'm outta here." And away Mo went. He was a man of decisive action.

Across the room, Willie threw his hands in the air so violently that he ripped the underarms of the jacket he was wearing. Tonight's color was purple.

"Goddamn, Milt. That's it between you and me! Don't let me catch you sneakin' and peepin' mo more!" And then the rage in his voice rang out in frustration, "Sheeeeeeeit."

Willie spotted Jack by the door and walked over. "Hey hey hey, ol' Jack. Well put together like a fine piece of leather!"

Willie was looking a little thinner. Jack had heard that he was sick, but he pretended not to notice. "Look Will, I'm cool with tonight. And hey, I'm leaving town but I'll stay in touch." Willie shook Jack's hand for the longest time, holding it deftly with his fingertips. "Well man, I'll be seein' ya down the road then. Come back and produce a record for me." His bulging eyes still glistened, and Jack felt that Willie would hang on long enough to see that happen.

Jack walked across the parking lot back to his car. It was dark and another jet passed overhead, giving him the same sensation as he had before.

A Mercedes pulled into a parking space near him, and a woman emerged. As soon as she walked into the light, Jack recognized her. "Cleo, what the hell are you doing here?"

"I'm living on this side of town now. Had to get away from that scene on the south side. I heard Willie was singing tonight and I thought I'd take a chance. This is kinda like my neighborhood bar now."

"You thought I might be playing here?"

"I've seen you in worse dives."

Jack spoke quietly, "I'm leaving town. Goin' home."

Cleo looked at him with an intensity that he had never seen in her before. "Jack, I did come here to see you. I have to get away from this life right now. It's gotten crazy, and I can't think straight anymore."

Jack held his breath and then offered, "I'm thinking about going to New York for a week before I leave."

Cleo smiled and asked, "Do you want a companion?"

Looking at that face, illuminated by the dull parking lot light, Jack had never seen anything so perfect. "Yeah, let's leave tonight."

Cleo spoke excitedly, "We'll leave now, with just the clothes on our back. We'll make it up as we go. One week, Jack. OK?"

Jack left his car in the parking lot and climbed into Cleo's Merc. He figured that his amp would likely be stolen from the back seat and maybe even his car would be towed, but at this moment, knowing what the next week would bring was more than worth it. He still had his bass. And more importantly, he had Cleo.